PB
ROW

For Laura and Debbie
P.J.
For Daisy
G.R.

Published in 1997 by Magi Publications
22 Manchester Street, London W1M 5PG

Text © 1997 Pippa Jagger
Illustrations © 1997 Gavin Rowe

Pippa Jagger and Gavin Rowe have asserted their rights
to be identified as the author and illustrator of this work under the
Copyright, Designs and Patents Act, 1988.

Printed and bound in Belgium by Proost N.V., Turnhout

ISBN 1 85430 287 6

What's wrong with Rosie?

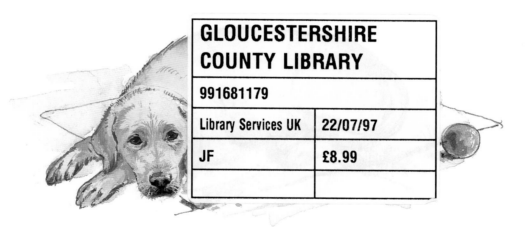

PIPPA JAGGER

Pictures by GAVIN ROWE

MAGI PUBLICATIONS

London

Nan's yellow labrador was eight years old.
She and Nan lived in a big square house deep in the Dales.
Rosie wasn't the best behaved dog in the world,
but to Nan she was very special.
She kept Nan fit by asking for walks before breakfast.
She kept Nan busy by leaving short yellow hairs and
chewed paper tissues all over the house.
And at night by the roaring orange fire, she kept Nan
company.

But Nan had a little worry.

Every six months or so Rosie would pretend she was having puppies. She would grow fatter and fatter and get slower and slower. And she would be particularly restless in bed, sniffing and panting and looking very tired. The first time Rosie played this trick Nan was completely fooled. She sat up all night in the armchair, in case Rosie needed any help with the puppies. But none had come and Nan wasn't fooled again.

And there never were any puppies.

There was just Nan's little worry that grew and grew inside her until it was as big as a headline and Nan could read it very clearly.

It said "ROSIE IS LONELY".

Nan wondered whether she should get a puppy for Rosie, but she couldn't decide.

One Friday in
March the phone rang.
It was Nan's daughter Jane
who lived on the edge of a big city.
"You must come over," she said.
"I've a surprise to show you."

Nan was excited.

Jane's surprises were always good.

Nan was so eager to be off she almost forgot to shut the garage door. She drove round the country lanes so fast that the postman thought she must be late for a wedding.

"In the kitchen," said Jane, the minute Nan arrived.

In the middle of the floor there was a large box.

In the box was a labrador with tired but peaceful eyes, and down her side was a squirming line of puppies, all having dinner.

Nan's legs felt weak.

She sat down.

"Bless them," was all she could say.

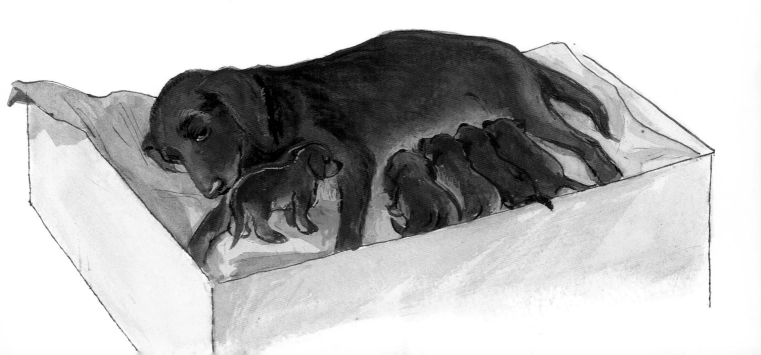

When the puppies were full
Nan picked one up.
It turned round and round
in her hands and pushed
its nose into her jumper,
mewing like a cat.

Nan watched the others falling asleep in the box and she imagined them growing up. In her head she saw crazy pictures, like a sofa with a huge hole in it, or a kitchen floor covered with scruffy, damp newspaper . . .

. . . or a walk in the lane before dawn and paw-prints on the rug.

Nan didn't ask Jane for a puppy. She went home alone, around the windy corners and over the rolling hills, back to Rosie.

March blew itself away and April stepped out brightly
under the cold sky.

Nan took Rosie for walks by the brown swirling river.
There were daffodils waving at the water and black-faced
lambs running in the sun.

Nan smiled at the Springtime but inside she felt uneasy.
One night, when she kissed the top of Rosie's head,
she hugged her very tightly.

"We've got each other," she murmured. "Isn't that enough?"
The silver hairs gleamed on Rosie's once golden face.

"Don't keep growing older," pleaded Nan. "Don't go and
leave me all on my own."

Rosie raised an eyebrow and made no reply.

Then one morning Rosie stayed in bed.

Nan laughed at her as she began to sip her coffee.

"I only got up for you," she said. "And look at you,
you lazy dog!"

Rosie lifted her head briefly and let it rest again.

She licked her front legs a bit but they wouldn't work.

Nan frowned. She washed, dressed and got the car out
before the coffee had cooled.

It was a strain getting Rosie into the car. Her yellow body
lay helpless in Nan's aching arms but her eyes did their best.

Nan laid her on the sheepskin rug and shut the hatchback
door. Then she was off.

In the village the vet was just unlocking his doors.
"Come straight in," he said. He didn't take his coat
off and he left the keys swinging in the lock.
"Rosie's very ill," he murmured. "I'm afraid
she needs an operation."
"Right," said Nan. She felt as though
someone had switched all
her lights off.

Nan couldn't remember driving home.
When she walked into the kitchen she picked
up the mug. It was cold like the stone wall in
the garden.

The day grew into a monster with a million arms.
Everywhere Nan went it tapped her on the shoulder and
whispered "How's Rosie?"
At teatime the phone rang. The vet said "We operated just
in time. I think Rosie should stay here overnight but she can
go home in the morning."
Nan just said "Yes, in the morning." Then her legs took her
to a chair and sat her down.

Rosie came home the next morning just as April was leaving. Nan treated her like a baby, washing her face, checking her stitches, mashing her food in case her teeth had gone soft.

"What would I have done without you?" she whispered into Rosie's ear.

She nursed her like this until she accidentally caught sight of Rosie through the porch window, rolling in the rose bed, laughing and kicking her legs.

"The cheek!" said Nan. "That dog's getting sneaky in her old age."

OLD AGE!

Those two words stabbed Nan in the chest like two stiff fingers on an angry hand. She knew what she had to do.

Nan got the car out.
This time Rosie jumped in the back
on her own and lay guarding all her doggy junk.
"To think I almost left it too late," said Nan, as she
watched the roads get straighter and busier, and the hills
turn into houses.
Eventually Nan stopped. She was outside Jane's house.
Jane was delighted.
"I knew you'd come," she said.

This time in the kitchen the big dog was sleeping and there were just two wriggling puppies, rolling over each other on the floor. One ran back to its mother but the other skipped and side-stepped all the way to Nan. It lifted its front paws up and down and its tail was a blur of fur.

Before she knew it, Nan had picked it up and put it on her lap.

It was soft just like silk.

It was warm like the smile of a friend.

It was love at first sight.

When Jane saw the tears in Nan's
eyes she made her a huge mug of tea,
and listened to her talking for a long time.
"Everything's going to be fine now," said Nan at last.
And a little voice inside her added,
" . . . for all of us."

Later, in front of a gentle fire in the big square house deep in the Dales, the puppy lay down, put its head on Rosie's back and fell asleep.

"Are you pleased?" Nan asked Rosie.
Rosie looked up. She opened her mouth to yawn
and to Nan it looked like a wide grin.
"Bless you both," Nan said.

May lingered in the lanes, and in the fields it grew green
grass for the dogs to roll on.
And Nan knew that Rosie would never play her puppy
trick again.

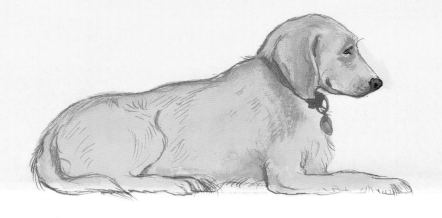